WHO HELPS ANIMALS?

by Erica Donner

TABLE OF CONTENTS

tadpole books

WHO HELPS ANIMALS?

A cat is sick.

A vet can help.

dog

A dog is hurt.

A vet can help.

A rabbit is sick.

A vet can help.

A lizard is hurt.

A vet can help.

bird

A bird is sick.

A vet can help.

horse

A horse is hurt.

A vet can help.

Who helps animals?

Vets do!

WORDS TO KNOW

bird   cat   dog

horse   lizard   rabbit

INDEX